VJ

The
Three Little
Witches

Hubble Bubble!

Look out for more storybooks by
Georgie Adams and Emily Bolam...

The Three Little Princesses
The Three Little Pirates
The Three Little Magicians
The Three Little Vampires

The Three Little Witches

Georgie Adams and Emily Bolam

Orion
Children's Books

ORION CHILDREN'S BOOKS

First published in Great Britain in 2006 by Orion Children's Books
This edition first published in 2010 by Orion Children's Books
This edition published in 2017 by Hodder and Stoughton

10

Text copyright © Georgie Adams, 2001, 2010
Illustrations copyright © Emily Bolam, 2001, 2010

The moral rights of the author and illustrator have been asserted.

A CIP catalogue record for this book is available from the British Library.

ISBN 978 1 44400 080 1

Printed and bound in China

The paper and board used in this book are from well-managed forests and other responsible source

MIX
Paper from
responsible sources
FSC® C104740

Orion Children's Books
An imprint of
Hachette Children's Group
Part of Hodder and Stoughton
Carmelite House
50 Victoria Embankment
London EC4Y 0DZ

An Hachette UK Company
www.hachette.co.uk

www.hachettechildrens.co.uk

For Mia Barclay Errington –
with love, G. A.

WOOD

MOUNTAINS

MOUNTAIN CAVE
where Baby Dragon
lives

CAULDRON
COTTAGE

where Zara, Ziggy
and Zoe live

where the shooting
star fell

BRIDGE END
where Tag, Tig
and Tog live

THE TREE HOUSE
where Mick
and Max live

KEEP
OUT!

where the
school ran
to one day

3

Contents

Chapter 1
Let's Have a Party! 11

Chapter 2
Zoe's Tidy Spell 21

Chapter 3
Wizard Wink's School 33

Chapter 4
Zara Cooks a Treat 43

Chapter 5
Ziggy's New Broomstick 47

Chapter 6
Shooting Star Magic 57

Chapter 7
Shopping at Whizzo's 65

Chapter 8
Party Night 73

Chapter 1

Let's Have a Party!

Once upon a time there were three little witches called Zara, Ziggy and Zoe.

Zara had a frog called Fidget.

Ziggy had a cat called Jelly.

Zoe had an owl called Two Hoots.

They all lived together in Cauldron Cottage, deep in Magic Wood.

One morning the calendar on the wall sang a little song.

TODAY'S BEGUN, THE NIGHT HAS BEEN –
NOT LONG, I SEE, TILL HALLOWE'EN!

"Hickety-pickety," said Zara.

"Hinks-minx," said Ziggy.
"I love Hallowe'en!"

"Wippety-woppet," said Zoe.
"Let's have a party!"

"Great idea!" said Ziggy. "We can send out the invitations today."

The three little witches made a wish list
of everyone they wanted to ask to their party.

"Wizard Wink," said
Zara.

"Baby Dragon,"
said Ziggy.

"Tag, Tig and
Tog Troll,"
said Zoe.

"Max and Mick," said Ziggy.

Then Zara said: "What about Melissa?"

"Oh, not that horrid little witch!" said Ziggy. "Remember when she turned Jelly into a frog?

Zoe crossed Melissa's name out. Slime green ink burst out of the pen and all over the page.

"It's a sign. She knows you've crossed her out!" cried Zara. "Put her back or there'll be trouble!"

Zoe wrote down Melissa's name again. It looked rather messy.

Then the three little witches got busy and wrote out all the invitations.

The invitations looked like this…

COME TO OUR
PARTY!

at......... Midnight ....

on ...... Hallowe'en ....

Tricks, treats and monster jelly!

Please reply to:
Zara, Ziggy and Zoe
Cauldron Cottage
Magic Wood

Then they addressed the envelopes like this...

Wizard Wink
The School House
Magic Wood

Baby Dragon
Mountain Cave
Magic Wood

Max and Mick
The Tree House
Leapfrog Lane
Magic Wood

Tag, Tig and Tog
Bridge End
Magic Wood

Melissa
The Webs
Which Way
Magic Wood

Next Zara chanted a spell:

HURRY NOW TO HOUSE AND DEN
AND BRING THE ANSWERS BACK AGAIN!

Each invitation sprouted tiny wings and fluttered off to deliver itself to someone in Magic Wood.

Chapter 2
Zoe's Tidy Spell

The little witches liked living in Cauldron Cottage.

Downstairs there was:

a den for games

a place to keep their broomsticks

a sitting room where they watched television

a kitchen

FUNKY FEET

Upstairs
there was:

a bathroom

three little bedrooms

ZARA'S ROOM

ZIGGY'S ROOM

BEWARE SPELLS

ZOE'S ROOM

Zara, Ziggy and Zoe each had their own
room, with their name on the door.

One morning the little witches were busy doing housework. They used some magic to help them.

BROOM, BROOM, SWEEP THE FLOOR.
DUSTER DUST THE SHELVES.
CUPS AND PLATES JUMP INTO THE BOWL —
AND WASH UP BY YOURSELVES!

But some of the magic went wrong.

Milk Jug squeezed too much washing-up liquid into the bowl.

The Taps turned themselves ON and squirted water everywhere!

The Teacups laughed so much, they got HICCUPS.

Hic!

And the Spoons had a lovely time playing with the bubbles.

The little witches found the kitchen floor covered in foam.

But it was fun to play for a while.

Then they mopped up the mess.

Afterwards Zoe went upstairs with Two Hoots to tidy her room.

Zoe sat on her bed. She had lost her Spell Book *again* and was trying to remember the spell for putting things away.

She closed her eyes and began:
TIDDLE-TUM TAY. MUDDLE WHIRL AWAY...
But before she could think of the next line a gust of wind blew her bedroom window open.

BANG!

Zoe's words had called up a twirly-whirly wind by mistake!

WHOOOOOOO.OOOO!

Her bed flew up to the ceiling.
"Wippety-woppet!" she cried.
Zoe's things whizzed about
faster and faster.

WHOOOOOOOOOO!

Luckily the spell soon wore off.

"My room looks worse than ever now!" cried Zoe. "I WISH I could remember that tidy spell…"

Just then Zoe's Spell Book landed on the bed with a THUMP!

"Tidy spell. Page forty-two. I'll read it," said Spell Book.

TIDDLE-TUM TAY. MUDDLE WHIRL AWAY. BIM-BAM-BOOM. TIDY UP THIS ROOM!

This time the spell worked like magic.

When the little witches had finished
their jobs, they sat down and watched
their favourite TV programme – *Weenie the
Wonderwitch!*

Time for
telly!

Remember those party invitations?
The very FIRST reply arrived
by special Crow delivery!
The little witches were very excited.

Special Delivery –
as the crow flies

To Littel Witchiz
Call Dron Cottage
Magic Wood

Dear Zara ~~Piggy~~ Ziggy Zoeee

Thanks for yor IN VIT A SHUN.
Cool! We will bee there.
From Max and Mick

P.S. We promiss not two
do any bad trix.

This is a pick ~~tuer~~
of our Tree House.
Hope you like it!

32

Chapter 3

Wizard Wink's school

The little witches go to Wizard Wink's school in Magic Wood. One morning while they were having breakfast the kitchen clock sang out:

**HURRY, HURRY, DON'T BE LATE –
OFF TO SCHOOL, IT'S HALF-PAST EIGHT!**

Wizard Wink's school was magic. It was in a new place every day.

"I wonder where we'll find it today?" said Zoe.

"We'll ask Signpost," said Zara. "Race you to the crossroads!"

Zara got to the crossroads first. "Please Signpost, have you seen our school?" she asked.

"Ah, yes! It ran by a moment ago down Leapfrog Lane," he said.

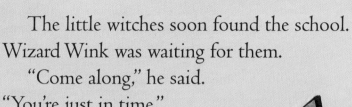

The little witches soon found the school.
Wizard Wink was waiting for them.

"Come along," he said.
"You're just in time."

Big Red Book called out the names of
everyone in the class:

"Tig!"

"Tag!" "Tog!"

"Baby
Dragon!"

"Mick!"

"Max!" "Melissa!" "Zoe!" "Ziggy!"

"Zara!"

"If I had three crystal balls in one hand…"
said Wizard Wink, "and four in the other …
what would I have?"

"BIG HANDS!" shouted Max and Mick.

"Oooh! I know!" said Zoe. "Seven!"

"Right!" said Wizard Wink.

"Poo!" said Melissa. "That was
easy-peasy."

Next they did some painting. Wizard Wink gave the class *magic* paints to make their pictures come alive:

HALLOWE'EN PARTY
by Zoe

MAGIC CAULDRON
by Ziggy

FROGS
by Zara

A WICKED WOLF
by Melissa

FIREWORKS
by Baby Dragon

MONSTERS
y Mick and Max

DIGGING FOR GOLD
by Tag, Tig and Tog

The lesson was going well until…

Ziggy's cauldron overflowed . . .

. . .the wicked wolf chased Zara's frogs

. . .the monsters messed up Zoe's party

. . .and Baby Dragon's rocket went
WHIZZ! BANG! all around the classroom.

WHIZZ! BANG!

Wizard Wink had
to wave his wand to
put things RIGHT.

"Now," said Wizard Wink, "I'm going to make a potion."

SLIMY FROGSPAWN, SLIPPERY SNAILS
MIX TOGETHER WITH LIZARD TAILS
TOE OF TOAD, EYE OF NEWT
BREW IT UP IN A SMELLY OLD BOOT!

He gave everyone a drop of the mixture and this is what happened:

I've SHRUNK.

I'm as small as Fidget.

I'm as tiny as a teaspoon.

It was great fun! When it was time to go home, Wizard Wink waved his wand and everyone grew again.

"See you all tomorrow," he said.

The crow brought the SECOND reply in a packet. It looked like this.

Ziggy followed the instructions.

★ ★ ★ ★ ★ ★ ★ ★
Instant Star Signs
★ ★ ★ ★ ★ ★ ★ ★
The brighter way
to send your message!
Just add water

★ ★ ★ ★ ★ ★ ★ ★

Instructions
★ ★ ★ ★ ★ ★ ★ ★
READ CAREFULLY
BEFORE OPENING.
1. Open packet.
2. Pour Instant Star Signs
powder into bowl.
3. Add water
4. Stand clear to
read message!

★ ★ ★ ★ ★ ★ ★ ★ ★

To Zara Ziggy Zoe

I'm coming so there! Melissa

Chapter 4

Zara Cooks a Treat

One afternoon Zara decided to make
something special for tea. She tapped
Cookery Book and said:

SAUSAGES IN BATTER!

Cookery Book called out all the things
she would need:

Milk!

Flour!

And...
TOADS!

Butter!

SAUSAGES IN BATTER

Eggs!

The things jumped onto the table
as their names were called.

Cookery Book said the word 'Toads' again and again just for fun.

Suddenly fat toads were all over the kitchen floor! Luckily, when Jelly came in, they hopped quickly away.

Zara shut Cookery Book before he could cause any more trouble.

She snapped her fingers and said a spell:

SPLITTER, SPLITTER, SPLATTER
SAUSAGES AND BATTER.
BAKE THEM IN A DISH FOR TEA
FOR ZIGGY AND ZOE AND ME!

Then POOF! A dish of sizzling sausages landed on the table.

"Tea's ready," said Zara.

"Brill!" said Ziggy.

"Wicked!" said Zoe.

*It wasn't long before the THIRD
reply arrived.
The crow brought the little
witches a note burnt with fire.*

Dear little witches
Thank you very much
for your invitation.
I can come.
Lots of love
Baby Dragon
x x x x x x x

Chapter 5

Ziggy's New Broomstick

One day while Ziggy was out flying, her broomstick went CRACK!

A few seconds later, Ziggy and Jelly crash-landed in Magic Wood.

"It's time I had a new broomstick," said Ziggy, rubbing her knee.

When they were back at Cauldron
Cottage, there was a knock at the door.
"Broomsticks for sale!" said a goblin.
"Ooh, just what I wanted!" said Ziggy.
It didn't take Ziggy long to choose one
called the Comet.

Ziggy took her new broomstick outside to try it.

Just then Max and Mick swooped down on their broomsticks to take a closer look.

"Cool," said Max.

"I'll race you!" said Ziggy.

"Great idea! Let's fly three times round Magic Wood," said Mick.

"First one back here is the winner!" said Max.

Ziggy put Jelly on the broomstick and climbed on.

"One . . . two . . . three . . . UP!" she cried.

They all tapped their broomsticks, and then they were off.

WHOOOOOSH!

3

Wow wheeee!

Ziggy's new broomstick shot up SO fast!
She raced ahead once, twice round Magic
Wood.

"Let's slow that broomstick down!" Max
shouted to Mick, as they went round for the
third time.

They waved their wands at Ziggy's broomstick, and it began to

shake,

fly sideways,

dive,

and do loop-the-loops!

"Having trouble?" shouted Max, as he flew by.

Ziggy guessed they had cheated. She decided to do some magic of her own.

Max and Mick were sure they would win the race now. But suddenly they looked down and saw a tree with sweets all over it.

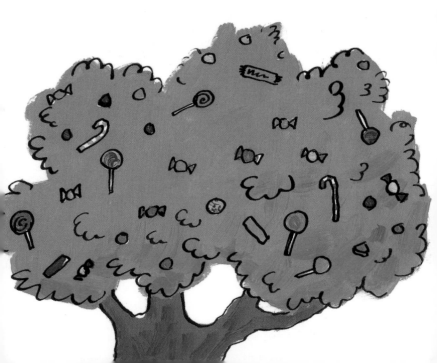

Max and Mick
loved sweets!

"Here we come!"
cried Mick.

The boys thought
they could stop for
a while – and STILL
win the race. But once
they started eating
Ziggy's magic sweets
THEY COULD
NOT STOP!

It wasn't long before Ziggy flew over her magic tree. She waved to them and called out,

"Can't stop. I'm in a race!"

"Oh no! The race!" groaned the wizard boys, as Ziggy sped to Cauldron Cottage and won the race after all.

The FOURTH reply was a
Spell-o-gram. One afternoon it fluttered in
through an open window.

Spell-o-gram   To Zara, Ziggy and Zoe

Cauldron Cottage, Magic Wood

Thank you

for your invitation. I should love to

come to your party   From Wizard Wink

Chapter 6
Shooting Star Magic

One starry evening the little witches were playing hide-and-seek with Baby Dragon and the trolls, Tag, Tig and Tog.

Ziggy was counting,

"...ninety-nine, ONE HUNDRED. Coming!"

Ziggy found Zara, Zoe and Baby Dragon easily.

But she couldn't find Tag, Tig or Tog anywhere.

Suddenly they heard a loud noise up above.

A tiny golden star came shooting from the sky.

"Let's go and find it," said Zara.

"*And* look for those trolls!" said Baby Dragon.

SWOOOOOSH!

Tag, Tig and Tog had forgotten all about hide-and-seek. They'd gone to dig for treasure instead. The star landed right by them.

"Gold!" said Tag.

"Treasure!" said Tig.

"We're rich!" said Tog.

"That's MINE!" said somebody else.

It was that mean witch Melissa.

"Give me the gold or I'll turn you hairy little trolls into toadstools!" she said.

"But it's ours," said Tag.

Melissa threw some magic powder at the trolls. But just then the little witches and Baby Dragon came along. The powder made Baby Dragon SNEEZE.

AH-TISHOO! AAH-TISHOO!

AAAH-TISHOOO!

The BIGGEST sneeze blew the magic powder all over Melissa and she turned into a toadstool.

Everyone fell about laughing.

Baby Dragon looked worried.

"Melissa will say it's all my fault," he said. "I'll be in BIG trouble!"

The little witches had an idea.

AAAAH-TISHOOO!

Zara picked up the star, Ziggy said a spell and Zoe blew stardust over the toadstool.

POOF!

"When the magic wears off, Melissa won't remember anything!" said Zara.

Baby Dragon WAS pleased. He thanked the little witches like this:

Thankyou very much little witches

Later when Melissa changed back from being a toadstool ... she didn't remember a THING!

At last the Crow brought the FIFTH
reply to the little witches.
It was a magic postcard from Bridge End.

GREETINGS
from Bridge End

POST CARD

Dear little Witches,
Thank you for your
invitation. We will be
there on the stroke
of Midnight!

Tag, Tig and Tog
x x x

To
Zara, Ziggy and Zoe
Cauldron Cottage
Magic Wood

Chapter 7
shopping at Whizzo's

On the day before Hallowe'en, the little witches went to Whizzo's supermarket to buy things for their party.

Whizzo's sold everything a witch could want. First the little witches went by shelves full of things for making spells.

SPELL MAKING

WORM JUICE

Lizard legs

SUN-DRIED BONES

FREE RANGE DRAGON EGGS

RATS

PICKLED BEAKS

SPECIAL MOONWEED

Delicious!

WORM JUICE

They stopped to look at some magic books and saw Wizard Wink. Their clever teacher was selling copies of his latest book *Spellbound*. The little witches bought a copy.

WIZARD WINK
will be signing copies of his latest book "SPELLBOUND" here today 1pm

Wizard Wink signed it for them. He wrote inside:

TO ZARA ZIGGY AND ZOE

WITH BEST WISHES FROM Wizard Wink

By now the little witches' trolley was nearly full. There was just enough room for some sweets.

Hallowe'en Fun

Suddenly Zoe gave a shout.
"Look out!"
Three large bats zoomed over
their heads.
"Amazing!" said Ziggy.
"Let's buy them," said Zoe.

But catching them
wasn't easy...

The little witches raced around, climbing
over cauldrons and falling over pumpkins
until they'd caught the bats!

Luckily the bats were so tired after all that flying, they folded their wings and went to sleep!

The little witches hurried to the check-out. Then they put the bats into carrying boxes and hurried out with their bags.

"What a whopping lot of shopping!" said Ziggy.

That night the little witches spent a
long time watching the bats. They could do
fantastic flying tricks…

wing to wing,

upside down,

and backwards!

Later the little witches counted up all the replies.

"Max, Mick, Melissa, Baby Dragon, Wizard Wink, Tag, Tig and Tog."

"Eight!" said Zoe.

"And US!" said Zara.

"Eleven!" said Ziggy.

"ZICKERY, ZACKERY, DOODLE-DO!"

Chapter 8

Party Night!

It was the day of the little witches' party!
Zara, Ziggy and Zoe were busy getting things
ready.

The calendar on the kitchen wall was very
cheerful. It sang over and over again:

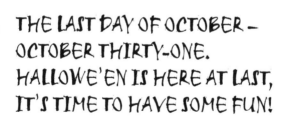

THE LAST DAY OF OCTOBER –
OCTOBER THIRTY-ONE.
HALLOWE'EN IS HERE AT LAST,
IT'S TIME TO HAVE SOME FUN!

The little witches sang along as they made crazy food for their party.

Cookery Book flipped his pages and called out recipes for:

Fudge feet!

Witchy fingers!

Toothy bites!

Monster jellies!

Bat cakes!

Beetleburgers!

They also put some laughing sweets in a dish.

I wish they were REAL.

Whoooo-arrh!

Afterwards they did the decorations.
Ziggy blew up balloons.
Zara sat the skeleton in a corner.
Zoe dangled spiders in the windows.
"It looks really spooky," said Zara.
"I wish it was midnight now!" said Zoe.

Zara looked outside. It was getting dark.
"Time for the lights," she said.

The little witches carefully lit candles
inside their pumpkin lanterns and hung
them outside by the door.

ELEVEN O'CLOCK, I KNOW THAT'S RIGHT — ONE HOUR TO GO BEFORE ... MIDNIGHT!

sang the clock.

"Have we got everything ready?" said Zoe.
"Everything except ... US," said Ziggy.
The little witches dressed up in their very best Hallowe'en outfits.

Just before TWELVE o'clock, they counted down the seconds:

Five! Four! Three!

Two! ONE!

The clock struck the first stroke of
midnight and everyone arrived on time.

BOING!

First they played Spot-the-Spook with the ghost the little witches had bought at Whizzo's.

WHOoooo-ARRH-oOOooo

The ghost drifted about,

popped up in strange places,

grinned ghoulishly

and gave them all a fright…

…until it discovered the laughing sweets.

After that it went:

OOO-hoo-hoo-hoo-HA-HA-HA!

so loudly everyone knew where it was!

Next Wizard Wink had a surprise.
He waved his wand and three pairs of silver
boots appeared.

"Try them on," he said to Zara, Ziggy and
Zoe.

The little witches pulled them on, then...

POOF! PUFF! PING!

Brill!

Wicked!

Magic!

The little witches
vanished.

Later, when she thought no one was looking, naughty Melissa tried a pair on. But she put the boots on the WRONG FEET!

She grew taller, and taller, and TALLER

"Help!" cried Melissa.

Wizard Wink quickly said some magic words, and Melissa was the right size again.

"And NOW it's time to EAT!" said Zara. She snapped her fingers and...

the toothy bites gnashed their teeth,

the witchy fingers beckoned spookily,

the monster jellies
waddled,

the fudge feet
danced,

the beetleburgers scuttled about

and the bat cakes flew round the room.

Catching and eating them was
the best fun of all.

When it was time to go home, everyone thanked the little witches for a lovely party. They all agreed it had been the best Hallowe'en party for a long time.

That night three tired but happy little
witches got ready for bed.

"Goodnight,   "Goodnight,   "Goodnight,
Zara"   Ziggy."   Zoe."

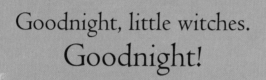

Goodnight, little witches.
Goodnight!

OOD

MOUNTAINS

MOUNTAIN CAVE
where Baby Dragon
lives

CAULDRON
COTTAGE

where Zara, Ziggy
and Zoe live

where the shooting
star fell

BRIDGE END
where Tag, Tig
and Tog live

THE TREE HOUSE
where Mick
and Max live

KEEP
OUT!

where the
school ran
to one day

Look out for
The Three Little Princesses

Tan-tan-terrah!

Meet Phoebe, Pruella and Pip.

It's the king's birthday but everything will go wrong unless the three little princesses can find the missing key to the magic clock.